For Popo
—L. B.

For Ah Gong
—J. K.

Published by Roaring Brook Press · Roaring Brook Press is a division of Holtzbrinck Publishing Holdings Limited Partnership · 120 Broadway, New York, NY 10271 · mackids.com · Text copyright © 2021 by Livia Blackburne · Illustrations copyright © 2021 by Julia Kuo · All rights reserved. · Library of Congress Control Number: 2020912213 · Our books may be purchased in bulk for promotional, educational, or business use. Please contact your local bookseller or the Macmillan Corporate and Premium Sales Department at (800) 221-7945 ext. 5442 or by email at MacmillanSpecialMarkets@macmillan.com. · First edition, 2021 · Book design by Jen Keenan · Printed in Malaysia by RR Donnelley Asia Printing Solutions Ltd., Shah Alam City, Selangor State · ISBN 978-1-250-24931-9 · 10 9 8 7 6 5 4 3 2 1

I DREAM OF POPO

written by **Livia Blackburne**

illustrated by **Julia Kuo**

我夢見婆婆

Roaring Brook Press
New York

I dream with Popo as she rocks me in her arms. She sings, "Beibei xin, beibei gan." In my heart I hear: My baby, my heart. My baby, my love.

I walk with Popo in the park, squeezing her finger in my chubby palm. When I wobble, she holds me up. She pushes me on the swing and lifts me to hear the birds sing.

I bow to Popo on New Year's Day. She asks if I've been good and gives me a red envelope. Then she fries up crispy, gooey, sweet New Year's cakes, so hot they almost burn my tongue.

I sit with **Popo** and she shows me where I'm going to live. Here is Taiwan, so tiny, surrounded by blue. There is San Diego, far, far away.

"You will learn and see many new things," she says.

I wave at Popo before I board my flight with Mama and Baba. The airplane thrums like the biggest cat I've ever seen.

"Fly safely," Popo says. "Call me every
week and tell me about your adventures."

I think of Popo as I meet new friends, kids with hair of every color and skin of every shade.

They say, "Hi."

I say, "Ni hao."

I talk to Popo from across the sea.

"I'm learning a new language," I say. "And I miss your dumplings."

"I'll make them for you when you visit," she says.

I draw Popo at my new school. Below the picture I write "My grandma," though it feels strange to call her that.

I learn other words, too:

Taiwan 台灣

dumplings
餃子

my grandma
婆婆

motorcycle
摩托車

home
家

taxi
出租車

San Diego 聖地亞哥

teacher
老師

school bus
校車

friend
朋友

new house
新房子

palm tree
棕櫚樹

After a while, the words form easier on my tongue.

I hug Popo when I come back to visit. Now "ni hao" is what feels strange in my mouth. Other words, too, are hard to catch, like fish in a deep well.

大中華888

547·XE

I ask Mama why I can't talk to Popo like before.

"You can still hug her as tight as before," she says.

I do. Popo hugs me even tighter.

I eat with Popo in her house, surrounded by the fragrance of gui hua blossoms. She cooks my favorite dumplings, dipped in soy sauce and sesame oil. Her house looks smaller than I remember, but everything smells the same. Popo looks smaller, too. Her hair is more white.

When I board the plane again, Popo
packs me dumplings to eat on the way.

I wonder how she'll look when I see her again.

I pray for Popo when we hear she is sick. I sing to her as she lies in bed, frail under heavy blankets. I wish I could reach across the ocean and hold her up.

She whispers to me in a voice soft as birdsong. "Beibei xin, my baby, my heart."

It's a promise and a kiss.

I dream of Popo coming
to me while I sleep.

I say, "Ni hao."

She says, "Hello."

I say, "Wo ai ni."

She says, "I love you, too."

A breeze brushes my face,
rich with the scent of gui hua.

I tell Popo about my adventures, and she smiles.

Although *I Dream of Popo* is fiction, I drew deeply from my own life to write it. Like the main character, I also moved to the United States at a young age, and like her, I found  it a big adjustment. Several decades ago, five-year-old me boarded a Boeing jumbo jet in humid Taipei. Sixteen hours and one layover later, I was running across the tarmac at the Albuquerque International Sunport. It was dark outside, and twenty degrees Fahrenheit. For a girl who'd never seen snow, it was quite a shock.

Everything was different. I went from subtropical mountains to high desert mesas, dumplings to enchiladas, Asian metropolis to American suburbia, giant flying cockroaches to . . . smaller non-flying cockroaches. (Not all the changes were bad.) More relevant to the story, I also went from seeing Popo (婆婆), Gonggong (公公), Yeye (爺爺), and Nainai (奶奶), several times a week, to calling them every few weeks or months. (International calls were expensive!) Because of the significant time difference, we usually called late at night, when it was morning in Taiwan. To this day, I can hum the tune a touchtone phone makes when dialing the long-distance code for Taipei.

Many of the details in this story will be recognizable to those familiar with Chinese and Taiwanese culture. The phrase *beibei xin, beibei gan* (貝貝心, 貝貝肝) was one my own popo often used with me. Literally, it translates to "baby heart, baby liver." In Mandarin, the liver is often used in conjunction with the heart to signify affection, the implication being that the person in question is as close and vital to the speaker as those inner organs, hence my interpretation as "My baby, my heart. My baby, my love." A more common phrase is *xin gan bao bei* (心肝寶貝), which is similar to "sweetheart" in English.

There are a couple of Chinese New Year traditions mentioned in this story. Children usually receive *hongbao* (紅包), red envelopes filled with cash, from their elders, often after the children show respect by bowing and wishing their older relatives a happy new year. When a young person marries, the expectation for red envelopes flips, and that person thereafter gifts envelopes to his or her parents.

Nian gao (年糕) is a sticky rice cake traditionally eaten during the new year. The Mandarin word for *sticky* (黏, pronounced *nián*) sounds the same as the word for *year* (年). The cakes can either be sweetened or cooked unsweetened in savory stir fries. I have a soft spot for the sweet variety dipped in beaten egg and pan fried.

The *gui hua* (桂花) blossoms mentioned in the story are also from my personal experience. *Gui hua*, aka sweet osmanthus, is a fragrant flower native to Asia. My popo had one on her balcony. For the longest time, my family knew it solely by its Chinese name, but a few years ago my mom caught a whiff of its very distinctive fragrance at a local botanical garden. It only took a bit of subsequent sleuthing to find *gui hua*'s English moniker.

When you live away from loved ones, memories of place get interwoven with memories of people. The humid musk upon exiting Taoyuan Airport smells kind of like a favorite childhood park. Carpets of moss on roadside gutters evoke memories of the steep road to Popo's house. And curls of steam off a street vendor's cart bring mouthwatering memories of morning walks to fetch rice noodle soup for breakfast. As anyone who has lived apart from family can attest, the sights, smells, and sounds of a beloved place become intertwined with the relationships they conjure, along with all the love and complexities that come with them.

I'm fortunate to have my own daughter now, and her world is much more connected than the one I grew up in. Videochat and broadband internet, though not a replacement for in-person visits, make it easier to keep in touch. Foreign movies, TV shows, and podcasts can now be streamed on the internet.

As my cohort of first-generation immigrants raise our own children, many of us are recognizing the value of our family languages and culture. We're trying to pass them on to our offspring, be it through language immersion schools (or recruiting grandparents to create their own "language immersion programs"), food, or travel. Many of my friends also speak gratefully about the close relationships their kids share with their parents (their kids' grandparents). It's a blessing to have and see that closeness, and it's not a blessing we take for granted.

ILLUSTRATOR'S NOTE

As a second-generation Taiwanese American growing up in suburban LA, my childhood memories were a mix of sunny pool parties, dreaded Saturday morning Chinese school, and unwavering love for Studio Ghibli movies. I had two sets of friends: my friends from school, and my Taiwanese American friends from Chinese school and church. The latter shared the same stories of rushed winter vacations or sweltering summer trips back to Taiwan, fighting jet lag to eat mango shaved ice or pepper steak buns and haggling for already dirt-cheap night market clothes.

There is a break in those memories. When I was four, my parents moved us to Taiwan for a year, thinking we might settle back down on the island. It was during

this stint in Taiwan that I went to my first drawing classes, transported on motorcycle by Ah Gong, my grandpa. I would crouch into a little ball between his legs, clutching my paper tube, as cars whizzed by. Over this year, I had Ah Gong's undivided attention, for better or worse. Ah Gong ran a steel parts shop downstairs and liked to tease me by asking me to fetch a customer's order from the aisles of heavy, unmarked steel tubes and parts. I would stumble from shelf to shelf, mortified, as everyone laughed. But I knew he loved me. He was always doting on me, making sure I sat next to him at the big dinner table, sneaking his favorite salty pickled cucumber, called *hua gua* (花瓜), into my bowl. He would spoil me by ordering *ou a jian* (蚵仔煎), or oyster omelets, from the famous shop next door even when our dining table was bursting full of home-cooked food. The dining table I drew in this story is what Ah Ma's (my grandmother's) dinners continue to look like every night, without fail.

When this year ended and we moved back to the States, I'd forgotten how to speak English! I had to relearn everything, and for a few years I would occasionally speak to my classmates in Mandarin before realizing my error.

Ah Gong passed away when I was in high school, forever to be associated with my childhood understanding of 1980s and 1990s Taipei. I've watched Taipei change in the time since, as my freelance career has enabled me to spend up to a month every year there since 2010. Instead of worshipping J-pop's reigning queen Ayumi Hamasaki, we are now ogling the newest K-pop groups. The streets are cleaner, and most squatting toilets have been replaced with Western toilets (a relief to many visitors). Cheese has been introduced to the Taiwanese diet in all sorts of curious dishes, and boy are they tasty. But there will always be reminders of Ah Gong. We still order oyster omelets every time I come home. Ah Gong passed his knack for small business on to my dad, who then passed it to me. And I love *hua gua* and all salty, pickled things, just like Ah Gong.

And now, as we sweep the dust off Ah Gong's grave, my thoughts move to my parents. I'm older than my parents were when they immigrated to the States. How hard it must have been to leave a place where they belonged, where they understood the world, and where they were understood! My parents were accosted by rowdy Halloween partiers before they knew what Halloween was. My dad's first car was a Toyota because a car salesperson couldn't understand his pronunciation of "Buick." And yet they thrived: They earned master's degrees, worked hard at their mom-and-pop shop, formed a community, and found a new religion. After all of that, after thirty years of adapting, they moved back to Taiwan to take care of ninety-four-year-old Ah Ma. Once again, they are an ocean apart from their family—this time, their children. I hope someday I will be capable of the same types of sacrifices for my future family. But until then, I'll continue to take the bridge my parents have extended for me to Taiwan.

GLOSSARY

婆婆 (pópó): Maternal grandmother

貝貝心, 貝貝肝 (bèibèi xīn, bèibèi gān):
Sweetheart (literal translation: baby heart,
baby liver)

你 好 (nǐ hǎo): How are you?

餃子 (jiǎozi): Dumplings

摩托車 (mótuō chē): Motorcycle

我 的 婆婆 (wǒ de pópó): My grandmother

家 (jiā): Home

出租車 (chūzū chē): Taxi

校車 (xiàochē): School bus

朋友 (péngyǒu): Friend

老師 (lǎoshī): Teacher

新房子 (xīn fángzi): New house

棕櫚樹 (zōnglǘ shù): Palm tree

桂花 (guìhuā): Osmanthus flower

公公 (gōnggōng): Maternal grandfather

爺爺 (yéyé): Paternal grandfather

奶奶 (nǎinai): Paternal grandmother

心肝寶貝 (xīngān bǎobèi): Sweetheart
(literal translation: heart liver precious baby)

紅包 (hóngbāo): Red envelope

年糕 (nián gāo): Sticky rice cake

黏 (nián): Sticky

年 (nián): Year

花瓜 (huā guā): Salty pickled cucumber

蚵仔煎 (ǒu-ā-jiān): Oyster omelet

Romanizations are based on the Hanyu Pinyin pronunciation system.

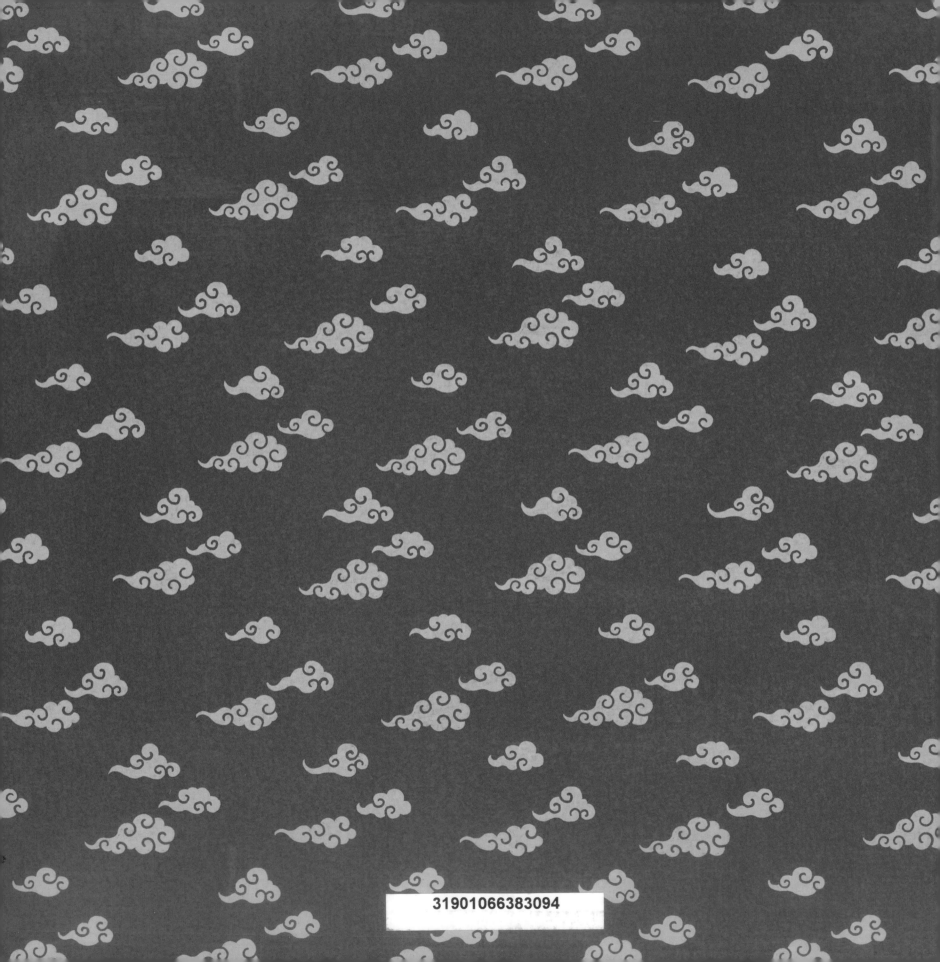